To Mom and Dad, Wife, Rustin Shiflet, Dr. Nic, Kaye Sinkule,
Shuli Green, Zac Brown Band, the Kameans, the Browns, and
the Branch family. And to Frances Gilbert and Random House,
Simon Green and CAA, Will Ward and ROAR, and Andy Elkerton.
—Coy

All rights reserved. Published in the United States by Doubleday,
an imprint of Random House Children's Books, a division of
Penguin Random House LLC, 1745 Broadway, New York, NY 10019.
Doubleday and the colophon are registered trademarks of Penguin Random House LLC.

Visit us on the Web! randomhousekids.com

Educators and librarians, for a variety of teaching tools,
visit us at RHTeachersLibrarians.com

Library of Congress Cataloging-in-Publication Data is available upon request.

ISBN 978-0-399-55286-1 (trade) — ISBN 978-0-399-55287-8 (lib. bdg.) —
ISBN 978-0-399-55288-5 (ebook)

MANUFACTURED IN CHINA
10 9 8 7 6 5 4 3 2 1
First Edition

When You're Feeling Sick

by Coy Bowles

illustrated by Andy Elkerton

Doubleday Books for Young Readers

Life has its ups

And life has its downs.

You have days when you smile,

You have days when you frown.

You have birthdays and holidays,
Good days and bad days.
The things that will happen,
Oh man, you'll be amazed.

But every now and then your body will get sick.

You get a cold, you get the sniffles,

You get something you can't kick.

GET WELL SOON

There are creepy-crawly bugs that can get inside your tummy.

They can make the food you eat seem not so very yummy.

You can get a virus, or the flu, or the itchy chicken pox.

And you curl up on the couch with a blanket and warm socks.

When you're feeling sick and feeling blue,

Here are some things you should not do.

If you follow these rules, you'll be just fine.

Here we go with the sickness guidelines:

Don't pour chicken noodle soup on your head.

It's made for your mouth and your belly instead.

Don't invite purple elephants over for lunch.

They will eat all your food and drink your fruit punch.

Don't feed your medicine to your cat or your dog.
They could turn green and leap like a frog.

Ribbit!

Don't be afraid of needles or your nurse.

She's not a wicked witch with a broom and curse.

(Nurses are the sweetest people in the whole universe!)

Doctors are the smartest people alive. They can count higher than one hundred and seventy ten zillion three billion and five.

Their job is to make you feel better and make you feel great

So you can get back to riding on your roller skates.

And whatever you do, don't give up.

I mean, dooooooon't give up.

Cuz if you do, you'll have to eat a chili ice cream Brussels broccoli sprout monkey-hair burger with green ketchup. So whatever you do, don't give up.

But if your hair turns blue and your toes turn into balloons,
And you flip upside down and float up to the moon,

Don't be sad all afternoon.

You will get well very very soon.

You're a hero, a champ, and even a trouper.

You're a black belt ninja of sickness.

You're super-duper.

You can beat anything that comes your way.

You can whup a ten-story, ten-legged, one-eyed, two-toed, four-armed, fire-breathing, huffing, puffing red-and-silver dragon—and even the sickness you have today.

So stick your pinkies in your mouth,

And your thumbs behind your ears,

And your pointers on your eyes—now PULL!

But don't make tears.

This is the sickness monster face.

If you wiggle your tongue and moan and groan,

Your sickness will leave without a trace.

If you do the sickness monster face and you still feel sick,

Then sing this Sickness Song and it will surely do the trick:

I feel sick and I feel poopy.

All this medicine makes me feel loopy.

So, sickness, sickness, go away.

Don't come again another day!

Whatever you do, you must stay strong.

You might be sick now but you won't be for long.

You'll be running and swimming and swinging

And playing and dancing and you'll feel just fine.

Don't you worry one little bit, it's just a matter of time.

Author Note

When I was a kid, my mom and dad used to take me to a restaurant called the Chick-fil-A Dwarf House. There was a tiny red door on the front of the building. I used to get so excited about being able to go in and out of a very small door that was made just for a little kid like me. I also had a very cool aunt who had a room built on her house especially for the kids in the family. There was a very small door that led into a full-size room with furniture that could have never fit through the tiny door. My imagination would run wild with this tiny-door portal to another world. I still view the world through those little doors at times, especially when writing children's books. As a writer of music and stories, I get so inspired by the creative brilliance of a child's mind. Rules don't yet apply to things like flying cats and dogs, monkey-hair burgers with green ketchup, and warding off a sickness with a song and a scary face.

When You're Feeling Sick comes from the deepest of all places in me. My mother had a health situation a few years back. My family and I sat for weeks in a hospital, patiently waiting for my mom to regain her health. I saw people come and go with good news and bad. This was my first experience of the fragile nature of the human experience. While at the hospital, I ran into someone I went to high school with. Her daughter had been battling a long-term illness for a while and was a fan of my first book, *Amy Giggles: Laugh Out Loud,* and the Zac Brown Band. Her mother said, "You've gotta come by and say hey and read your book to her. We brought it with us." This would be the first time I had ever read my book to a child, and I was so